T0121090

THE LOST ISLAND
of
ALTRONIA

CHRISTINE CARMONA

authorHOUSE®

AuthorHouse™
1663 Liberty Drive
Bloomington, IN 47403
www.authorhouse.com
Phone: 833-262-8899

Published by AuthorHouse 06/17/2021

ISBN: 978-1-6655-2836-8 (sc)
ISBN: 978-1-6655-2835-1 (e)

Print information available on the last page.

This book is printed on acid-free paper.

Part I

Chapter 1

Once upon a time, about 15 to 20 thousand years ago, when the lost continents of Atlantis and Lemuria still existed, there was a small island situated between Atlantis and a bigger continent to the west of it we know of today as America, called Altronia. It existed somewhere east of where the Bahamas are now.

This island, like Atlantis and Lemuria, was inhabited by a very highly civilized people. They knew how to do almost everything we know how to do today, except that they did a few things differently. While Atlantis was known for its crystals (which people then used for electricity, as well as medicine, among other things), and Lemuria was known for its successful harvests of the most diverse fruits and vegetables, Altronia was known for its accurate and long-lasting PC-boards (yes, they even had computers in those days).

On the center of the little island, there thrived a huge PC-board manufacturing plant. Everyone who was in the employment age worked at this factory, except sailors, builders, and of course the King and his family.

The people in this factory were pretty much like a family, except that they didn't act like it. They worked and socialized in small cliques, just like people do at school and work today. The names in this story have been translated into English for easy pronunciation and memory.

King Seabourne was the King who ruled the whole island. He behaved like a typical king would. He treated his subjects fairly. Everyone respected him. He ran his island justly.

His daughter, Princess Poinsettia, was always flying around in her aircraft. It ran on a crystal. The King bought the craft as a birthday present from the Atlanteans. She was the only girl on this island to own one. She often flew it to her boyfriend David's compound to visit him. Every weekend they'd go roller skating at the local skating rink. You would typically see the couple skating together, hand in hand.

Poinsettia was the King's only child. He had no son.

King Seabourne was a very powerful king, but he was getting very old. People knew he would retire soon and were contemplating on who should be his successor.

One of the people who wanted King Seabourne's throne was Monkey. He came from a family who included Things among its members. Things are descendents of humans who were genetically engineered with animal DNA, or animals with human DNA, like the centaur, the winged people, etc. So the monkey wasn't completely human, but his immediate family had got rid of most of their animal traits by choice mating, praying, meditating, and laser surgery, but he still had some of the mental inheritances of a monkey. That is how he got his name. Nevertheless, he was the only one in his family lucky enough to get the same basic education the humans got. He worked at the PC-board company, drilling holes in the boards. He possessed a fair amount of humor and amused many people around him.

One of the people very amused by him was Dianna, a young girl who lived on Atlantis, but who often traveled to Altronia because of her work. She was an interior decorator and went around painting the insides of people's caves and dwellings red, black, gold and orichalcum. Orichalcum is the best form of bronze. The Atlanteans had total control of this product. They got it from one of their colonies. They were the only ones in the world you could get it from. So she painted the caves and buildings like they wanted in those days and when asked, she'd also paint frescoes on their walls. She had a lot of work to do in the Factory (they wanted their walls painted, too). And that's how she met Monkey.

This relationship started when Monkey's boss introduced Dianna to him one day, at his workplace. As he led Dianna into the room where Monkey worked, the latter was just lamenting, "Oh I'm so tired of this job!" to which his boss replied, "I don't wanna hear it!" Then he said to Dianna, "Dianna, this is Monkey," as the latter was just shutting down his drilling machine for lunch. Then his boss said to him, "Monkey, this is Dianna. She just recently started working with us."

"Oh," said Monkey. "When did you start?"

"The day before yesterday." answered Dianna.

"Which circle are you working in?" asked the Monkey.

"I'm working all over," said Dianna. "You see, I'm an interior decorator by trade, and King Seabourne's got me painting the interior walls of this building."

"I see," said Monkey, "It's about time those walls get painted. They've got pretty dirty and are even showing cracks in some places. They need painting!"

"Yes," said Dianna, "and he's even letting me paint a fresco in the Chief's office!"

"You can do that too?" asked Monkey.

"Yes," boasted Dianna, "In fact, that's what I like to do the most!"

"Well, I've got to go have lunch. Have fun!" said Monkey as he waved and left. His idea of lunch wasn't exactly just eating a bowl of rice. He also liked to smoke a joint too, as he called it, "to get my head together."

On another day, Dianna was climbing out of her balloon, which was her way to get around. She was just going on her break. On some breaks she'd go see Monkey. She was experiencing a hard morning, and she wanted to have something to laugh about. "Hi, Monkey!" she said, as she walked into the drilling and routing room. "What's goin' on?"

"What's up?" he'd say.

"Nothin' much." She'd say. "How's your day goin'?"

"Okay, did you say you were from Atlantis?" asked Monkey.

"Yes." Dianna answered.

"Where in Atlantis?" he asked, prying further.

"From Poseidon, you know, where the big harbor is."

"And how long have you been livin' on Altronia?" he asked.

"I'm still living in Atlantis." Dianna said.

"Then how do you get here every day?" he wanted to know.

"I travel in my balloon airship!"

"Every day?"

"Sure!" said Dianna, "It's not that long of a trip, and the scenery is great!"

"How does it get propelled?" he asked.

"By this 24.9-volt crystal. It's not much, but it gets me here and back."

On another day, Dianna was going to the Kiva Nova to take her lunch break. As she approached the door, a bunch of guys came gushing out. The last one was bouncing a ball. It was Monkey. So Dianna went in and said to one of the guys who was still there, "Some people will do anything to keep themselves busy at lunch time!"

The guy laughed, because he understood exactly what and whom she meant. In those days, people were able to read each other's mind, just by tuning in to each other's frequency of vibration. Besides, he had just seen Monkey bounce the ball around himself. Sometimes, when all the guys are there at the Kiva Nova, they have a practice game of hip ball in the courtyard, which was in the middle of the restaurant and had an open ceiling and roof. When Dianna happened to be there, while they were playing, she'd watch.

There were other times when she'd bring along her lyre to play at lunchtime. One of those times, shortly after she started working on Altronia, a young guy, who also played the lyre, brought his in, and they jammed together in his aircraft during lunch. They played the newest

Atlantean song that had just come out on the wall. Their music sounded beautiful and was mesmerizing several of the Altronia inhabitants who happened to be around there that day.

Altronia had its fleet of ships which carried the PC-boards to its neighbors, including Atlantis, the mainland (America), and Lemuria (Mu), and traded them for what they had: high-tech things and natural drugs and spirits from Atlantis, fruits and vegetables from Lemuria, and crystals the Atlanteans mined in what we know today as America. These ships were being led by the Great Captain Boofy. This man was extremely good-looking and the wisest and nicest person in all Altronia. He had a kind of charisma unlike anyone else and treated his workers firm but fair and everyone liked him. He also knew his profession better than anyone; he knew the waters so that his crew would never get lost or stuck in any eddy. He never sank a ship in his life. And when his ship would arrive at a harbor and it's time to unload the products coming to Altronia and load up the products going to the foreign land, he was the only captain who would get off his ship and help his workers.

One of the times when the ship from Altronia docked at the Altronia Harbor of Atlantis, and while the Great Captain Boofy was helping his workers, Dianna, the interior decorator, was walking toward the harbor. She liked her career and found her assignment quite interesting. However, she was dissatisfied about one little detail. She was thinking, 'Where are all the good-looking men on this island? There don't seem to be any here!'

But once she arrived at the harbor, she was about to change her mind. Just then, at 12:00 o'clock, she saw a man with shoulder-length, almost straight black hair, cut in layers into "a shag" with split bangs. He was the most beautiful man she'd ever seen! He looked like a god to her. She said to herself, 'Wow! Who's that sailor over there? I've never seen a guy like that before. I must meet him!' He was tall, had an athletic figure, almond-shaped eyes, long eyebrows, long straight aquiline nose, and a goatee.

From that day on, every time the C.S. Altronia (Crystal Ship Altronia) docked at Altronia Harbor, Dianna was right there, standing ready, waiting to see Captain Boofy.

For many months, she'd only look at him, without saying anything. Sometimes he'd look up from his work, sensing that he was being watched, and see her, but that didn't stop her from looking at him. So he would just resume working without reacting.

When Dianna was on the Island of Altronia, she usually ate lunch at the only restaurant on the island, called "Kiva Nova". Today, she got a pleasant surprise. Captain Boofy sat there on one of the hay bails in a corner with some of his sailors, also eating lunch. At this time, Dianna decided she's had enough of just looking at him. She walked over to them and asked, pointing to an empty space on a hay bail, "Can I sit here?"

An older man, who was eating some strange concoction that the restaurant waiter served as that day's special, said, "Sure, have a seat!"

Now I know that it was not a custom of the Atlanteans or Altronians for a woman to sit at a table with a bunch of men. But that didn't stop Dianna. So she sat in a round circle in the restaurant between two of the sailors, across from the captain. However, now that she was sitting right in front of Captain Boofy, she felt a little nervous at first. She said with a forced smile, "How're you all doin'?"

"Okay. So what's your name?" asked the one sitting to her left.

"Dianna. What's yours?"

"Rusty." he said.

"Where are you from?" asked the guy to her right.

"I'm from Atlantis." said Dianna with a smile.

"What brings you to Altronia?" asked another sailor.

"My balloon. I'm here on a business assignment." said Dianna.

"What kind of a business assignment?" asked Captain Boofy. Dianna looked at the captain for a second before she answered, "I'm an interior decorator by trade and the King has assigned me to paint the interior walls of the big PC-board plant on this island."

This had all the sailors exclaiming, "Oh wow!"

Dianna went on to say, "He's also got me painting a fresco in the Chief's office."

That elicited another exclamation from the sailors: "Wow!"

Captain Boofy said, "Let me know when you're done so I can check it out!"

"Sure, I will." said Dianna. Then she asked the crew, "Are you the fellas who come to Poseidon's Harbor and drop off P.C. boards once in a while?

"Yup!" said one of the guys.

"Really?!" exclaimed Dianna. "What's the name of your ship?" she asked. "I know it starts with a CS, but I never got to see the rest of the name." she said.

"It's called the 'Crystal Ship Altronia'." said one of the sailors.

"We also deliver software programs!" said one of the other sailors.

And then Captain Boofy said, "Yeah, we deliver a lot of things!

Now Dianna started asking him questions, starting with: "What's your name?"

"I am Captain Boofy!" he said, raising his eyebrows, lowering his eyelids, and putting his hand on his chest.

"Ahh, and I am Dianna!" she said in a less conceited manner. "How long have you been sailing ships?"

"Oh, for about seven years now!" he answered.

"Oh really," said Dianna, "and do you like this profession?"

"I wouldn't be doin' it if I didn't!" he said.

Eventually they got to talking about music. "What groups do you like?" asked Dianna.

"I like Rush, they're the best!" said Captain Boofy, looking very educated.

"I like Rush, too!" said Dianna, "Do you play an instrument?"

"Yes, I play bass lyre." said the captain.

"Oh cool!" said Dianna. "I play the regular lyre. We should get together and jam sometime!" Dianna loves to play music with other amateur musicians.

Just then, it was time for the guys to return to work and for Dianna to return to her wall painting. As she started to paint again, following that interesting break she just had, she felt kind of strange. She thought, 'Hmm, what's going on with me? My lips are tingling, my heart is pounding, and this guy at the restaurant is on my mind like crazy! I feel like I'm hot all over!" Yup! Dianna had just fallen in love with the captain of the Crystal Ship Altronia, Captain

Boofy! Now she knew her life would never be the same again.

This started a series of Dianna playing her lyre at the Kiva Nova whenever the sailors had lunch there. She played covers of songs, including a few of that group called Rush, Captain Boofy's favorite band, like 'Trees', which she learned recently from the guy she jammed with in his craft the other day, as well as her own songs, including Beyond & Back, which at the time was only an instrumental song. The lyrics came much later. So there she sat, in the corner, on a hay bail, playing her lyre, while Captain Boofy and his sailors sat somewhere nearby, talking and eating lunch.

Later, after lunch break was over, and the sailors were heading back to the ship, Dianna asked Captain Boofy, "Hey, Captain, how did you like the music I played? I put in some songs by your favorite band, Rush!"

"I heard them. You played very well!" he said.

That inspired Dianna to bring in her lyre more often and play it in front of the captain. 'Hey, maybe I could make a career of this!' thought Dianna.

Meanwhile, in Atlantis, every time the C.S. Altronia would sail into Poseidon Harbor, Dianna and Captain Boofy would meet and talk for a while.

"Hi, Captain Boofy!" said Dianna.

"Hi." said Captain Boofy.

"What're you doing?" asked Dianna.

"Loading up the ship." answered Captain Boofy.

"Mind if I help?" suggested Dianna.

"No, go ahead!" said Captain Boofy.

Dianna picked up a few smaller, lighter boxes and handed them one by one to Captain Boofy, who quietly took them and handed them to the next sailor in line, who in turn passed them to the next sailor in line, etc., till the last one put it on a parcel elevator to the guy on the ship.

Dianna had a blast helping Captain Boofy. Before long, they got the cargo loaded up and it was time for Captain Boofy and his crew and ship to depart. "See ya next time, Captain!" waved Dianna.

And so it went for a few weeks. Whenever the C.S. Altronia would dock at Poseidon Harbor or Altronia's harbor, Dianna, who had its schedule pretty much figured out, was sitting right at the dock, waiting for the ship to come in. While she'd be helping with the loading, she and Captain Boofy would have conversations together. He'd tell her stories about the seas and the other harbors where he had to go. She'd tell him stories about Atlantis.

In one scene, Dianna said, "Hey, Captain Boofy, have you heard, Rush is playing at the Poseidon Theater in June!"

"No, really?" said Captain Boofy.

"Yeah," said Dianna, "Are you going?"

"I dunno." answered Captain Boofy. "I'll hafta see. Maybe."

Another time Dianna saw Captain Boofy, she said, "Hi, Captain Boofy! How are you?"

"I'm kinda pressed for time today. The last harbor we stopped at, we had a big load to drop off, and it took an awful long time to unload. Plus the dock manager was talking to me and carrying on --- he just wouldn't stop talking. Eventually I hadda tell him we needed to be in Poseidon Harbor by half-moon the next month, so we had to get moving."

"Oh," said Dianna, "and which land was that?"

Captain Boofy said, "the Land of Og."

The isthmus in Panama, Central America, had a small waterway going through, which people with powerful abilities, like Captain Boofy, were able to make temporarily big enough to sail a ship through. That's how Captain Boofy's ship was able to sail from Atlantis to Lemuria (on the other side of the globe, in the Pacific Ocean) and other places, like Peru, Easter Island, and Egypt.

One day, while they were talking on the dock, a horrendously loud, shrill voice yelled, "CAPTAIN BOOFY! YOU GET UP HERE RIGHT NOW!!!" Both the Captain and Dianna were shocked but Dianna more so. They looked up on the ship. There was this fat, old, ugly woman looking down over the deck, her face red with anger.

"Who is that, Captain Boofy?" asked Dianna in whisper voice.

"That is my wife." answered the Captain nonchalantly.

Now Dianna was even more shocked. "You mean," asked Dianna, fighting back her tears. "You're married?"

"Yes." said Captain Boofy resignantly.

Dianna ran away, her face hidden in her hands.

For a whole week after that day, Dianna did nothing but cry. She couldn't go to work; she tried to play her lyre, but nothing could take her mind off of what she found out about Captain Boofy. So severely did it sting!

Captain Boofy had 2 major friends on Altronia: one was Monkey, the other was Athol. The latter also wanted to inherit King Seabourne's throne. He was tall, muscular, very macho, not as good-looking as he thought he was, a real narcissist. He had an ego that went too far and kept him from sustaining any relationship with women. He loved women, although only for their bodies. Anyone who met him soon found out that he was so vain that it was very difficult to have any long conversations with him.

What Athol did for a living was masonry. He was the chief of the island's construction company. Through his hard-working men, whom he forced to work often long hours for days on end, he built many beautiful temples, housing complexes, and even pyramids. These buildings had very thick walls, not only to mitigate earthquakes, but also so the neighbors couldn't listen in on people's conversations and couple's fun.

Some buildings were made of enormous slabs of rock and granite. His workers used sound frequency to move them. They knew how to create an anti-gravity field by raising the frequency of each rock to the frequency of gravity, which is 1012 Hertz. At this frequency, the rock loses its weight and becomes airborne. They also would turn the edges into an almost liquid gel to make them fit exactly to each other so that they didn't need to use mortar between. He and his workers also built roads out of giant slabs of rock and tunnel walls out of huge bricks, put together so tightly that one couldn't even stick a knife in between them.

Yes, Athol's men were excellent masonists, but they led hard lives, for their boss often drove them to faint in exasperation. That's what a slave driver he was. But King Seabourne liked their work so whenever he wanted a temple, shrine, or palace built somewhere on that island, he'd contact Athol.

Every now and then, when Captain Boofy, Monkey, and Athol all had a night off, they'd get together and party until late in the night. Since Captain Boofy's wife, Lorelei, was a very jealous woman, he always had to take her along, because she wouldn't let him go anywhere – work or play – without her. Athol and Monkey would sometimes fly off the handle and get rowdy with each other or with others, but Captain Boofy would always behave so he earned the respect of other men and the adoration of women, although his wife wouldn't stand any other woman looking at him.

Chapter 2

Back in those days, people liked to play certain games, such as for instance a game called "Hipball", which was similar to soccer, except instead of hitting the ball with the foot or the head, they can only hit it with their hip. The players wore a protective ring around their hips so that the pelting of the rubber ball doesn't cause too much pain. The citadel, or field in which it is played, usually had a vertical ring hanging high up un the wall, and the players had to somehow get the rubber ball through the ring, which was very difficult, especially since the players were not allowed to touch the ball.

The ladies loved to watch the men play this kind of sport. Dianna was working on her wall mural when a couple of guys from the CS Altronia came by to tell her about the upcoming

Altronia Hipball game. One of them, Rusty, said, "Dianna, are you going to the hipball game?"

"What game?" asked Dianna.

"The hipball game!" said Rusty.

"What's a hipball game?" asked Dianna, since she'd never watched one played before, although it was a popular sport at that time.

"Well," explained Rusty, "hipball is a game in which the players move a ball to each other and up and down the field and through the ring on the wall by hitting it with their hips. They're not supposed to touch it with their hands."

"Oh!" said Dianna. Then she asked, "Who's going?"

"The employees of the PC plant on Altronia and the sailors of the CS Altronia."

"Is Captain Boofy going?" asked Dianna.

"I'm pretty sure," said Rusty. "He is usually one of the players!"

"Okay, maybe I'll go." said Dianna.

"You should!" insisted Rusty. "See, many of us get stoned on a certain herb before we get there, and some of us are so stoned by the time the game starts that they can't see the ball.

When we say, 'get the ball', they say, 'what ball?'"

Dianna laughed and said, "In that case I'd better go!" And so the boys talked her into going to the hipball game.

The sun was high in the sky as Dianna walked with many people down the path to the citadel, where the game was to be held. When she arrived, there was already a number of people sitting on the steps surrounding the field (actually, it wasn't a field, as the ground was paved with large plates, like a patio, but larger). Among those people were Captain Boofy and his wife sitting close together, heads bent toward each other, down in the front row.

Dianne didn't feel too comfortable about seeing her there. She seemed to look better now. It was plain to see that she was pregnant. Captain Boofy, as well as his friends, was in the game. He was just sitting there, waiting for the game to start.

The game could not start until after King Seabourne would hold his speech, ending with "Let the game begin!" Then the players streamed onto the playground. They got into position, the "umpire" would throw the ball into the field, and the game began. The players ran from one side of the field to the other, hitting the ball with only the hip. If a player hits it with anything else by accident, he gets disqualified. Now, as Rusty warned Dianna, the players often have a buzz on by the time they arrive at this event, because they just got done with a week's work and this game always gets precluded by a round of the special herb taken by the players (and Captain Boofy's wife). So quite often, someone would hit the ball with the wrong body part and get promptly disqualified by the umpire. Also, the players would often hit the ball into the wrong direction, where no one was standing, so someone would say, "There's no one standing there!" or "Were you hitting it to a ghost?" The spectators got plenty to laugh about. Sometimes a player would get hit in the wrong place (the soft spot) and would find himself lying on the ground in fetal position in pain and embarrassment. But that didn't happen this day.

Captain Boofy seemed to be quite serious about the game. After the game was over, he asked what the score was, just to make sure. When someone told him, "26," he yelled, "26?!?"

The game winded down as more and more players got disqualified and sent out of the field. With less and less players remaining until only two remained, the crowd started cheering whoever they wanted to win. The players that remained were Captain Boofy and one of his sailors. Captain Boofy often wins these games and when he doesn't win, he usually gets a very high score. He almost won today, but in the last minute, he got so excited that he forgot to hit the ball with his hip and happened to touch it. The umpire saw it and the crowd went, "Awwww!" Too bad! Dianna would have loved to see him win. So would have his wife. Oh well, there's always next game!

The next day after the hipball game, Dianna saw Captain Boofy at the shipyard. She said, "That was an exciting game yesterday!"

"Aw, thanks!" he said.

"You know," continued Dianna, "your wife looked pretty yesterday!"

"Really?! Yes --- yes, I know. Thanks." he said, "You see, she used to have real long hair --- long silky hair, all the way down to her knees." he continued, "Then one day, I think it was the day before our wedding, she went and cut it all off!"

"She did? Why?" asked Dianna.

"I dunno. I think she said she was trying to copy the hair-do of one of the famous actresses. It was such a pity!"

"How much did she cut off?" asked Dianna.

"It was almost up to her shoulders after she cut it off."

"Gee, that is a pity!" said Dianna. "She should have saved it."

"Yeah, but I don't think she did." said Captain Boofy.

"I also noticed she's pregnant." said Dianna. "When is she due?"

"Anytime between 2 weeks from now and one moon." said Captain Boofy. "If you see me squirting to my ship, you'll know it's time!"

"Who will be the mid-wife?" asked Dianna.

"We will get Master Charge to help us with the birth." said Captain Boofy.

"Oh, I didn't know men were getting into this profession!" said Dianna.

Chapter 3

It was at the Kiva Nova where Captain Boofy sat with his sailors when Dianna walked in with her lyre. She nodded at Captain Boofy as she made her way to her corner. She sat down and began to play her music. Suddenly a man in manager clothes (what they wore back then) approached her and told her something, turned around on his heel, and split. Then she got up, looking mad, took her lyre and left.

Outside the door, she sat on the steps and played her lyre there. One could tell by the way she played that she was furious. Later on, Captain Boofy & Company came out of the restaurant and he asked Dianna, "Why are you playing out here instead of inside?"

"This (expletive) went up to me, said he's the new manager and that he doesn't let anybody play his instrument in his restaurant. Who is he to call this *'his* restaurant'?"

"Yeah, they changed managers just this week. I dunno; if I were you, I'd fight it, because you play pretty good." With that he left, followed by his crew.

Dianna wondered how she was to begin fighting this restaurant management.

The next Friday, Dianna had another challenging day. It started out like any other day. Dianna, whose travel balloon was getting old and starting to have a problem here and there, just got off from work and was looking forward to a restful weekend. She climbed into her balloon, started it up, and floated off to Atlantis.

Halfway there, about 50 knots before the island, her balloon started losing air. Her crystal that powers the aircraft had lost its charge for some reason, and it was completely discharged, like a toy out of battery power. So the balloon couldn't stay in the air any longer, since it had no power and not enough air. She could have sung a certain note to even up the frequency of the craft with that of the gravity, but before she had time to do that, the balloon had already made up its mind: it was taking a nose dive and crashed into the sea. Dianna somehow had already sensed that there was something wrong as she was leaving, so she put her parachute on just before she left, just incase. 50 feet before the craft hit the water she jumped out and pulled open her parachute after a few seconds. She landed far enough away from the balloon to prevent it from doing harm to her.

Hitting the water, she quickly removed her parachute and swam out from under it. Then she looked around to see where she landed and how far from Atlantis she was. Alas! There was no land in sight, nothing but ocean as far as her eyes could see. She landed too far from Altronia and nowhere near Atlantis and she wasn't sure if she could swim all the way to either shore. 'Darn!' she thought, 'right when I wanted to be home on time! Now what am I supposed to do, all wet, in the middle of nowhere? How am I supposed to get to Atlantis now?!'

Just then, a distant ship appeared on the horizon. "Alright! A ship!" exclaimed Dianna. "I hope it's one of ours!" She did the belly-up float to keep from getting too tired too early while she waited. As the ship drew near, she recognized it. It was the C.S. Altronia!

"Yesss!" Dianna got elated when she saw that ship. She had begun to get weak by then, even though she was only floating. Now she suddenly found the strength to start swimming to the ship.

As she reached within a mile of the ship, there was Monkey, aboard the ship, looking through some binocular-like instrument when he spotted her. "Hey, Captain Boofy," he shouted, "look over there at 3 o'clock!"

"What do you see?" asked Captain Boofy.

"It's a --- it's a --- it's a small head in the water --- it's a girl!"

"Lemme see!" said Captain Boofy as he took the instrument and looked through. Well, I guess you're right, Monkey! There is a girl struggling over there! Hey, I think we know her! It's Dianna!"

"I think we should save her!" said Monkey.

"I agree!" said Captain Boofy and ordered him to "...get the rope ladder out!"

"Eye-eye, Captain!" said Monkey who ran to get the equipment.

Seconds later, they were pulling Dianna in toward the ship. Carefully Captain Boofy and Monkey pulled her up and on board. She was huffing and puffing and when she was able to get enough breath to speak, she said, "Hooo! Thank you so much for saving me! I almost thought I wasn't going to make it!"

"You could never have made it to shore from back there!" said Captain Boofy.

After a day or so, when she fully recovered, Dianna went up on board to the rudder where Captain Boofy was nonchalantly steering the ship. He gazed dreamily over the ocean. "Hi!" she said to him.

"How're you doin'?" he said back.

"Better now. Thanks." she said, while also looking at the calm ocean, "Isn't it beautiful!" she exclaimed.

He was humming the song we know of today as "Peace of Mind" by a group of shoreline musicians from Atlantis, called Boston. He had been humming it when she arrived. It was one of her favorites. He was acting cool, calm, at ease, as if nothing was bothering him at the moment. "What's beautiful?" he asked, apparently in a daze. His wife wasn't around this time. She was at home, expecting their baby to come any day now.

"The wide-open ocean!" she said excitedly. "You can look wherever you want and all there is is wide-open ocean. And it's so peaceful!"

Captain Boofy side-glanced at her, raising his already high eyebrows, "Yeah, but the ocean isn't always this peaceful."

"How do you navigate your way around out here?" asked Dianna.

"Very carefully." said Captain Boofy.

"What do you mean by 'very carefully'?" asked Dianna, not being satisfied with that answer.

"Well see, it's not just a matter of turning this rudder to the left and right," said Captain Boofy matter-of-factly, "you also have to know all your nautical measures and how to use the looking-glass, you must know all the constellations and other stars and planets, …"

"Why?" asked Dianna.

"Because the sky is your reference map." explained Captain Boofy. "It shows you where you are and which direction you have to go in to get to your destination."

"Sounds pretty complicated." said Dianna. "--- Alright! Teach me, I want to learn!"

"You can't mean that!" said Captain Boofy.

"I *do* mean it!" exclaimed Dianna, nodding her head.

So he began to teach her how to navigate and sail a ship while she listened intently. The two looked like they were having a wonderful time.

Before long, the ship reached Poseidon Harbor and Dianne thanked Captain Boofy and Monkey for saving her and bringing her to Atlantis. While she walked back to her compound, where she lived, she felt about 60 lb. lighter, as if she was on cloud 9, or on the moon. She skipped a little, did some loops, singing that song that Captain Boofy was humming on the ship. She sang that song the whole way home. Yes that made her day: getting saved by Captain Boofy and sailing on his ship, watching him man the rudder. It was just lovely!

On another day, while Dianna was on the island of Altronia on another assignment, she was taking a walk on her lunch break when she passed by the shipyard where the sailors were loading up some PC-boards to go to Atlantis, or some other land. Among the sailors was Captain Boofy, who was diligently helping them. So Dianna went over to talk to them.

"Hi, guys!" said Dianna.

Captain Boofy stretched his lips and said "Hi." That's how he always greeted Dianna.

Some of the other guys said hello, too, and then went right back to work.

"Hey, how's it goin'?" Dianna asked Captain Boofy.

"Not too bad." he answered as he kept on working.

Dianna was ready to help again. So she asked, "Where are all these boxes going?"

"On the ship." was Captain Boofy's answer.

"I know," laughed Dianna, "but to which land?"

"Atlantis and a few other places." said Captain Boofy matter-of-factly. Then he asked, "You crash any more balloons lately?"

Dianna answered, "No. How 'bout you?" she asked, "Have you ever run into anything with your ship?"

"No. But I used to have a little flying aircraft, called the Camaro Z28!" he said with a smile. Then he continued with "I wrapped that around a tall palm tree."

"Oh wow!" exclaimed Dianna, trying to hide her smile. "Did you come out of that alright?"

"Yeah." he answered.

Dianna said, "I know you love your job. But what do you like to do when you're *not* working?"

"You wouldn't wanna know." he answered.

Dianna didn't expect that kind of answer, so she didn't ponder on the subject any further. Instead, she picked up a box and put it in the same pile as they put the other boxes, near the ship, where one of the sailors grabbed it and raised it onto the ship. While she did this, she asked, "Mind if I help?"

"Not at all, pitch in!" said Captain Boofy.

'He's so cool!' Dianna thought to herself, and picked up another box, handed it to him, he handed it to the sailor nearest to him, and on to the last one by the ship who sent it up on the ship. He hoisted it up without an elevator or rope or pulley system. He simply used his mind and some anti-gravity device. And so she was helping whenever they talked while he was

Christine Carmona

working. If something was too heavy, they'd use their minds to make it seem lighter. Helping each other, they soon had all the boxes on board the ship, except one. As Dianna reached for that box, Captain Boofy said, in pure sailor language, "f… it." That's because it contained trash and they didn't need to transport that.

Now that they were finished loading up the boxes, Captain Boofy said, "Another job well done!" and he climbed aboard the ship and waved good-bye.

There was a time when the people of Atlantis were expecting a delivery of fresh ginseng and because of an epidemic, a lot of people bought them to use for healing purposes (as far as is generally known), so now they were all out of ginseng and were in desperate need of another shipment from Lemuria via the C.S. Altronia.

"Let's go!" said Captain Boofy, as the sailors pulled up the anchors and the C.S. Altronia left Lemuria and once again set sail for Atlantis with a huge order of ginseng aboard among other things. There were dark, ominous clouds looming in the sky to the east.

36

"It looks like there's a storm brewing!" one of the sailors told Captain Boofy.

"S...t, looks bad!" said Captain Boofy, "But we must leave; the Atlanteans are waiting for their ginseng. If we leave now, we may be able to avoid it."

And so they sailed off into the East, while the sun was just setting in the West.

Two hours later, the air thickened. Soon the gusts of wind started tearing at the sails. The sailors have seen many a storm, but they've never seen anything like this, so they began to panic. One of them went to Captain Boofy, pleading, "Captain, we've got to turn back! Half the crew is scared, some aren't feeling good ... if we don't turn back, I have a feeling we are going to lose our cargo ---" by then, the ship had started rocking and tilting more and more; the rain had started pounding the deck; and half of the sailors were getting sick and were hanging over the railing; "... and maybe also a few men!"

But Captain Boofy was calm and cool. He knew how to handle the situation. He said, "Go and gather all the cargo, food, and fabric! Bring it below deck and then secure the hatches, the boat, extra yards and swivel guns!"

"Eye-eye, Captain!" said the sailor and did as he was told.

Just as the sailors were getting the last few things below, the heavy raindrops turned into sheets of water. The deck has become slippery and the sailors were sliding everywhere and falling down constantly. Up above, lightning was threatening to light the masts on fire. The ship was tossing and turning helplessly among glistening mountains of water in the raging storm, which was now not only making them late, but also trying to shred the whole ship and send it all, including its crew, to the bottom of the sea.

But no matter how bad the storm got, Captain Boofy remained calm and collected. Now the storm was ripping the sails off the masts. Captain Boofy had to yell to be heard above the howling of the storm. He yelled to the nearest sailor, "Get up there and take that sail down!" and as he was busy doing that, "And *you* get up *there* and take *that* sail down!"

They were somewhere in the middle of the sea when the storm tore the sail off the center mast. One of the sailors ran to Captain Boofy and yelled, "Captain, I'll go take *that* sail down!" and before Captain Boofy could say anything, the little sailor was climbing up the pole, which was swaying to and fro. It took him a while to detach the sail. Just as he detached it, lightning struck the pole and broke it in the middle. The little sailor went flying toward the deck at an enormous speed. Captain Boofy saw that, sprinted over to where he was falling, and caught him, though the catch sent both of them falling on the deck. But luckily neither one was injured beyond some scrapes and bruises. Then, looking at the broken mast, which was leaning on the railing, Captain Boofy ordered "Quick! Grab onto that end of the mast! Swing it this way! --- Okay, put it down here (next to the other half)!" and as they put it down, "Now go down and find us some rope!"

Five minutes later, that sailor came back with some rope. The Captain smiled briefly as he took the rope. Then he tied the broken-off part of the mast with the half still standing. He then ordered a sailor to climb up the still-standing half and tie the broken half to the standing half. The sailor put about one foot or two of the broken-off half to an equal length of the still-standing mast, side by side, and tied the two together. "Okay now," said Captain Boofy, "four of you sit around it, chant that the pole will stay up, and lean back against it!" It was a very challenging experience, but they managed to hold it up throughout the rest of the night.

The following morning, all was calm and the sun was shining when the sailors woke up, yes, even the ones holding the mast up. Captain Boofy was navigating the ship, like nothing happened the night before. At the usual morning meeting, he asked while smiling, "Alright, who's still livin'?"

The expeditor at Poseidon Harbor was following the weather reports and knew the C.S. Altronia was going through a rough storm and was worried whether it would arrive at all or not.

As the C.S. Altronia sailed in to Poseidon Harbor, (it didn't arrive too much later than expected), the expeditor was glad to see it arrive and when Captain Boofy climbed down the ladder hanging from the deck of the ship, and walked up to the expeditor to greet him, before he and his sailors started unloading the ginseng, the expeditor told him, "Captain Boofy, you amaze me!"

One day, at Poseidon Harbor in Atlantis, as Captain Boofy's ship came in, Dianna waited at the dock holding a little black box in her hands. As the "boys" debarked the C.S. Altronia, she asked one of them, "Where's Captain Boofy?"

"He's comin'; he should be down here soon!"

Minutes later, Captain Boofy came climbing down the ladder. "Hi, Dianna! What's up?" he said.

"I have something to show you." she said.

But before she had a chance to open the lid, Captain Boofy and Rusty jumped the equivalent of 4 feet high and ran away to hide behind the bushes, where they lay flat of the ground, on their stomachs, face down, with their hands over their heads.

"Where did you go?" asked Dianna, completely surprised and confused. "What do you think this is, a bomb?"

Then they slowly came out from hiding.

"This is no bomb!" she said, "Don't worry, you're safe!" She shook her head at their reaction. Then she gave Captain Boofy the box.

Carefully he opened it. "Ooohh!" he gasped. It was a crystal ball with a motor inside which made it rotate.

"I made it!" said Dianna proudly.

He switched it on and let it rotate a few turns. "Oooo!" he exclaimed, "Hey guys! Come check this out!" The whole crew showed up to look at Dianna's model. They were ooing and aahing too, especially when they heard that Dianna made it. "What is it?" asked Captain Boofy.

"It's a model of a Wankel engine." said Dianna.

"A what engine?" asked Rusty.

"A Wankel engine." repeated Dianna and she began to explain how it works. "It's a model of a rotary engine and it works without pistons or piston rods or a cam- or crankshaft. It's called Wankel engine after the guy who invented it."

"Neat!" said Captain Boofy. "Did you just make that last night?"

"No," laughed Dianna, "I made it a few years ago at an internship for crystal-making."

"Where did you do that?" asked Captain Boofy.

"On the Big Land, (meaning what is now America) where they make crystals." said Dianna.

Dianna was carrying a heavy basket of fruits that she bought from what we know as the fleamkt. She was carrying it on her head as was customary for the women to do in those days. But because of that, she couldn't look down without dropping the whole thing. The road she was walking on was a cobblestone street. Therefore, she couldn't see that one of the cobblestones was worn down, and as she happened to step on it, her foot turned over.

"Rats!" she said to herself, "This is the last thing I need, especially since I'm in a hurry to get home!" Although it felt somewhat uncomfortable to feel her foot suddenly turn over, she didn't feel any pain right after that, so she continued to walk home, her basket of fruits balanced on her head.

But once Dianna arrived home and sat down, her ankle started throbbing --- and swelling up to twice its width. Eventually the pain got so bad that her mother said, "Dianna, you'd better go to the medicine man and have him take a look at your ankle!"

So Dianna went to the temple where the medicine man stayed and treated, and sometimes cured, ailing people. He said, "Where's it hurting?"

"My ankle hurts." said Dianna.

"How long has it been hurting?" asked the medicine man.

"Ever since my foot overturned 3 days ago." answered Dianna.

"Well, let's take a look." he said.

Dianna put her foot on the wood stump. The medicine man looked at it from 3 different angles. Then he took a bundle of sage, lit it, and danced around Dianna while waving the burning sage in the air. That's called smudging. Then he used electro-magnetic energy to heal her ankle. He took a rose quartz crystal and put it on her ankle lightly and went into a trance for about 15 minutes. Dianna felt an enormous heat wave in her ankle while he did this. He also wrapped her ankle in bandages soaked in a special solution of herbs to expedite the healing. Then he let her go and told her, "Okay, you should come back for treatment every 3 days. And I recommend you stay off your foot for at least a week!"

"But I can't ---" Dianna started to say when the medicine man interrupted her with "Or walk on these crutches!" as he gave her a pair of crutches to walk on.

The next day, Dianna still went to work on Altronia, but this time with crutches. At lunchtime, she limped over to the shipyard, which happened to be near the place where she was working, to talk to Captain Boofy. When she didn't see him among the working sailors, she asked one of them, "Where's Captain Boofy?"

He said, "He's still on the ship." and seeing her with crutches and bandaged foot, "What did you do to your foot?"

"It turned over when I accidentally stepped on a worn cobblestone." she said.

"We have an elevator." he told her. "We use it to lift very heavy stuff. I could take you on board the ship with it, if you'd like."

"That would be great!" she said. So up they went on the ship's elevator, which runs on a crystal in the control room. When they arrived at the top, it placed them on board, and then he led her to Captain Boofy.

"What ch'ya doin'?" she asked him.

"Painting." he answered. He was painting the railing of the ship. His hair has grown to a thumb-length below the shoulder and was looking real nice and shiny, Dianna was noticing.

"You get to paint your ship, too?" she asked.

"Yep! I get to do everything!" he said. Just then he saw her on crutches and her foot in bandages. "What did you do to your foot?" he asked.

"I twisted my ankle." she said.

"Well, shouldn't you be at home resting your foot so you can walk again?" he asked, behaving like a father.

"I have a lot of work to do that needs to be done by the end of this moon phase, so I've decided to come to Altronia anyhow."

"Yeah, but how do you paint murals while on crutches?" he asked curiously.

"I do the best I can." said Dianna, "I just paint the lower part of the wall and leave the higher part for later, so I won't have to go on the ladder. Besides, I'm feeling a lot better since I got to see you!"

At that comment, Captain Boofy turned around and looked at Dianna for a second, then continued with his work.

Just then, Dianna looked at her timepiece and gasped, "Oh, it's already this late! I have to get back to work! See ya!" She turned and hobbled back to the elevator, rode down to the ground level, and hobbled back to her workplace.

Part II

Chapter 4

One evening, as it was getting dark and the first stars started twinkling in the sky, Dianna was getting ready to leave Altronia to fly back to Atlantis, to her home. It was way past the end of workday, but she ended up working late that night. Now she was almost ready to leave, when she saw a row of people heading her way in the distance. They looked shadowy until they got close enough so she could recognize the leader of the pack. It was Captain Boofy! 'Great!' she thought, 'I wonder where they're going!'

An entourage of people, mostly men, but also some women followed him. They were carrying beer kegs and other party stuff. So Dianna asked, "Hey, where are you going?"

As soon as they heard that, Monkey answered, "Ha-ha, I told you she'd want to know!"

And then Captain Boofy answered in his usual low voice, "My place."

Too bad he was married, and Dianna wasn't invited, otherwise she'd join them.

At Captain Boofy's, the party was quickly getting underway. The people gathered in a circle and played some kind of marble game, using small crystals instead of marbles. They did this after they passed around and smoked a peace pipe, you know, to get into the right mood. Usually, every time they got together, they'd all take a few hits off the peace pipe, first thing.

It would always happen that after a while of beer drinking and crystal tossing, Monkey and Athol would get rowdy and often start fighting in the circle, only to be interrupted by Captain Boofy, who would always say, "Hey, take it outside, men!" Then they would go outside and really fight --- until they'd get all bloodied up. The next day, they'd be best of friends again. Usually one would blame the other for cheating. "Hey, no cheating, Athol!"

"I wasn't cheating, you're cheating!" Monkey would say.

"No, *you're* cheating!" Athol would say. And so on and so on it would go, on and on, until they'd both end up outside, kicking and hitting each other bloody. This is why they never had any women.

The morning after one of those parties, Dianna and Captain Boofy saw each other on her way to work. Dianna asked, "So how was your house bash last night?"

"It was cool, … same as usual." said Captain Boofy.

"Do you have a lot of parties like that?" asked Dianna.

"Just about every weekend." was the answer.

"Can I come to one of your parties?" asked Dianna, having seen that there are also women at his parties.

"I dunno, we'll see." was his answer.

So they went their separate ways.

At the factory, the bosses were growing increasingly dissatisfied with Dianna's work. Even the other employees were tattle-tailing on her, reporting what time she'd come in, which was often late, due to talking to Captain Boofy on the way there. One worker even saw her talk to or watch him at Altronia Harbor and finked on her about that. Another time, she stopped to talk to Captain Boofy, but he wasn't there. Instead, someone else was there, saying he was the assistant Captain, the co-captain, or something, and he didn't tolerate Dianna anywhere near the ship, saying something like, "You can't be here! You don't have sailor clothes on or insurance or nothin'!"

Needless to say, this put Dianna in a bad mood to begin with, and her work suffered accordingly that day, or it didn't help her work any. One day, as she went to the ship, looking for Captain Boofy, she saw Monkey instead. He said, "Heyyy, what's up?"

"Not me." said Dianna. "Do you go to Captain Boofy's bashes often?"

"Whenever he has 'em." said Monkey.

She tried to play on the old days, when he was still interested in her.

"I wonder what it's like at these celebrations!" she said.

"I'll take you there one of these days!" he said.

He never did.

There were many hipball games on the Island of Altronia and Dianna went to every one of them, once she was made aware of them and knew she could see Captain Boofy there. Here is the story of another one of those meets.

The day was perfectly sunny, the sky cloudless. The players were warming up on the field as the spectators were accumulating on the benches. This field had the benches built in as wide stairs all around the field, which was sunk into the ground by about 4 feet. The people called it a citadel then.

As Dianna arrived, most of the "benches" were already full. Captain Boofy and his wife sat in the front row at one side of the field, their heads leaning toward each other, as usual.

Dianna sat down where she could find a space and watched the game quietly. On the field, the umpire pitched the "ball" from the middle of the field. The other players ran for it; one of them bounced it off his hip, and so the ball flew back and forth from one end of the field to the other. The players kept the ball moving and off the ground by bouncing it off their hip. If it did fall to the ground, the umpire would step in, pick it up, and throw it up in the air; and then one of the nearby standing, or more like dancing players would send it in the horizontal direction towards his team's goal by hitting it with his head.

After practice time had ended, the King said, "Let the games begin!" Captain Boofy joined the players, so now he, Monkey, and Athol were all in the game. Captain Boofy showed up with his arm in a sling, so he could only play with one arm. But in this game, arms weren't needed to keep the ball moving, so he could still play. Nevertheless, once he managed to get the ball straight into the ring from the center of the field. Everyone on his team and the sympathetic spectators cheered loudly. Then one of the players on the other team said, "Hey Boofy, what was that?" to which Captain Boofy yelled, "That was a sling-shot!" The others laughed.

Another time, one of the other players on the opposite team sent the ball to someplace next to the goal, where no one was standing. "We don't have any ghosts on our team!" joked Captain Boofy.

Meanwhile in the "bleaches" Mrs. Boofy was acting like a child, yelling out her husband's name 3 times, as if they were king and princess. She was telling all their friends how Captain Boofy got his arm in a sling: "… and then he just popped his elbow …" while she was wagging her elbow, "… and so we had to go to the Temple where the medicine man popped it back in!" She explained this over and over, and so happily, almost as if she was glad he dislocated his arm to begin with. Either way, one could see that she was overjoyed to get all this attention, as she was just thrilled to be his wife. See, they had been married only for a few months, so she was still experiencing that wedding bliss.

Dianna wasn't interested so much in the ball games. She couldn't care less about where the ball went. She was only there to watch Captain Boofy. Of course, she didn't sit next to his wife. She knew that would be too risky. So she sat in the next row, just close enough to hear the conversations they were having with their friends.

That game went over without much more excitement. It was somebody from the PC-board manufacturing plant who won that game.

It was the ninth hipball meet. It took place on Atlantis this time. Dianna had been looking forward to going to this game all month.

However, when she arrived, she noticed that everyone she knew on Altronia and from the CS Altronia was there – everyone but Captain Boofy. His sailors were there. His friends Athol and Monkey were there. But he himself and his wife weren't. They had always showed up at every hipball game. This was the first one they didn't come to. Dianna was so disappointed that her face grew longer and longer as the event rolled on. Eventually she got up, walked over to his friends, and asked Monkey,

"Hi Monkey, hey, would you happen to know where Captain Boofy might be?"

"Yeah, Dianna, he's not feeling very well." said Monkey.

"Aww," said Dianna, "so sorry to hear that. What's ailing him?"

"I dunno, but he's decided not to attend the game this time." said Monkey.

Upon hearing that conversation, Athol offered, "Hey Dianna, don't be sad, cheer up! I'll tell you what: why don't you go with me behind the bushes for a 'roll in the hay'!"

Dianna didn't find that comment very amusing and she fled in tears. She ran as far as she could away from all the people and hid behind a bush to cry. She cried so loud that she couldn't hear that Athol was following her. Silently, he watched her cry for a few minutes. But instead of feeling sorry for her, it seemed to turn him on in some nasty way. It seemed like she'd never stop crying. And the longer she cried, the more the silent stalker got turned on.

Then suddenly Athol couldn't stand it any longer. So he surprised Dianna. She looked up in horror as he attacked her. She tried to run, but he wouldn't let her. He was just about on top of her when she gave him a good strong kick in the soft spot. He didn't expect that and was so surprised that he reeled back a little and froze. She got up as fast as she could and ran. But she didn't get very far before he recovered from his blow and grabbed her by her hair. She reached over her head, grabbed his head, and with a strong thrust, she bent over, throwing him over her shoulder onto the ground in front of her. Then she gave him a few swift kicks and punches until he was almost unconscious. Then she ran like the wind back to the crowd, her dress partly in shreds, which were blowing behind her.

As Dianna arrived at the crowd, she told the first person she reached about what had just happened to her. She exclaimed between puffs and pants, "Excuse me, I had just been raped! I need your help!"

The news spread through the crowd like wildfire. Soon, a couple of Captain Boofy's sailors, Rusty and another sailor showed up and asked Dianna, "What happened?" After she told them, they dashed off in the direction she had come from. As soon as they reached Athol, they beat the culp out of him.

Meanwhile, the first woman and her husband to whom Dianna told what had happened were consoling her as they walked her home. Dianna was crying hysterically. The woman consoled her while the man kept cussing the perpetrator up and down, swearing him to eternal damnation.

When the 2 sailors found him, they stood on either side of him and the taller one said, "Hey, where do you think you're going, you stud?"

"Hello, dudes!" said Athol with a gleam in his eye, "Hey, guess what I just did!" And he went on to brag about what he did to Dianna, as if he were proud of it!

"Oh yeah?" said Rusty, the shorter one. "Well, how would *you* like it if someone were to give you one of *these?*" and he gave him a right hook.

"Or one of *these?*" said the taller guy and gave Athol a left hook. And so they carried on, beating the rapist into oblivion. They left him face down in the dirt, unconscious.

Hours later, Athol regained consciousness and went to tell Captain Boofy. He told him at a pub near the harbor, where the ship C.S. Altronia was anchored for the night. He walked in, his face bloody from the beating. Captain Boofy was just downing another goblet of genuine Atlantean ale when his friends made him look toward the door. Athol was a horrible sight!

"My godz! What happened to you?" Captain Boofy asked.

"Some of your sailors just beat me up, and for no apparent reason!" he answered, looking innocent. But Captain Boofy had already heard the news about the raping and who was the victim and that Athol did it. However, for now he continued to act as though he were still his friend. He took him to his ship to the hold (below the deck) and had his wife treat his wounds.

Once they were in the hold, Captain Boofy asked Athol, "Alright, I know about this already. So why did Rusty and the other guy beat you up?"

Athol answered with a smile, "Didn't get her all the way, but it was fun getting her at least this far!"

Captain Boofy couldn't believe what his friend had just said, but he said nothing.

The next morning, Captain Boofy went back on deck first thing at the crack of dawn and called all his sailors together for a meeting.

As the sailors all stood on deck in front of Captain Boofy, he said, "Alright, I found out that some of you had badly beaten up a friend of mine, Athol. Which of you done it? Step forward now, so I won't have to punish all of you!"

Slowly Rusty and the taller guy that beat up the villain stepped forward.

"Okay, you guys, I want you to scrub the deck with your bare hands for the next 3 days. Now GET ON IT!" Captain Boofy yelled, as the 2 guys ran to get rags and soap and water to scrub the deck.

Then he went into the hold to see how Athol was doing. His wife was already there, and they were engaged in a lively conversation. He had her in hysterics. Captain Boofy asked him, "It sounds like you're feeling much better!"

"Yeah, much better." Athol answered.

"I see!" said Captain Boofy.

"Well then," said Athol, getting up, "I guess I'd better go. The girls are waiting for me!" and he used the ship elevator to let himself off the ship.

After Athol was far enough away, Captain Boofy said, "Yeah right! What girls?" Then he went back on deck and called the 2 sailors to him that he sentenced earlier to 3 days of deck scrubbing. "Hey guys, you're relieved from your sentence!"

The sailors looked up into the Captain's face with open eyes and eyebrows raised, said, "You mean … we don't hafta scrub for 3 days?"

"Yes," said Captain Boofy, "that's what I mean. I understand why you beat up Athol. He had it comin' to him. Now go do your regular chores!"

They did so, smiling.

Chapter 5 A

Yes, there were many hipball games. Dianna went to every one of them. At the 8th annual hipball meet, she couldn't help but overhear that Captain Boofy also participates in Archery. That inspired her to definitely want to see him play that. So she asked one of the sailors, "Where is he playing next? And When?"

"You can ask him that yourself!" answered Rusty.

She turned around --- and there he was --- like a knight in shining armor --- in all his beauty! She asked him the same question, expecting him to say that he doesn't want to tell her, because his wife might be against her being there to watch him play.

But instead, he calmly said, "I'll be playing beyond the fish-tail hill, where the big megalithic rock meets the sun at sunset."

"Uh-huh, and when? I mean which day?" asked Dianna.

"At full moon!" was his answer.

"You don't really mind if I come watch?" asked Dianna to make sure.

"Nah." he said, assuring.

Dianna was pleasantly surprised.

However, her good mood didn't last long. On the day and in the place where he said the archery match would be, she put on her beautiful white dress and jewelry and made sure she would arrive on time, but when she got there, her heart sank. The whole field was empty. There wasn't a soul in sight! The only noise she heard was the crickets chirping. Dianna said to herself, "I'll cry later. Right now, I'm way too mad!"

She went to the pub where Captain Boofy always stopped for a brew after a tour at sea. It was the pub from which the archery team was formed. She asked the bar tender lady, "When will the archery meet be held?"

The bar tender lady said, "When the sun is in *this* part of the sky (pointing to a certain part of the ceiling), and the moon is in *that* part of the sky (pointing to a different part of the ceiling) and is in its quarter."

When the day came, Dianna put on her nice white gown again and some of her best jewelry and went to the field where the archery match was to really take place. This time, there were people sitting on one side of the field. Some of them were making a picnic out of the event. They had their blanket spread out between them, decked with various foods to which the family members helped themselves while watching the game.

As Dianna walked past the spectators, looking for a good place to sit, someone whispered, "Oh s..t!" She turned around. It was Captain Boofy, who was sitting next to his wife. Dianna had no idea how much her appearance upset Captain Boofy's ever jealous wife. She sat down behind the couple, but left a good distance between them and herself, so to try not to upset things more than they already are.

One by one, the contestants went up and fired their arrows. Then it was Captain Boofy's turn. He shot the first arrow and missed the middle but hit the outer ring. His eyebrows went up while his eyelids went down, like he was feeling a stabbing pain. His second arrow did the same. Again his eyebrows went up while his lids went down. The third one went right in the middle of the target and the crowd went, "Ohhh!"

His comment, "That's more like it!" As the other competitors got up to shoot their arrows, he made comments like "Archer, archer, fire!" or "Ready, steady, aim, fire!" or "Come-on, fire that thing!" or "Are you going to fire that thing *today*?" anything to make the other archers nervous and miss their target. At one time, way back in Atlantis' old days, the participants used to be respectful and quiet during the shooting of the arrows, but that was long ago. Since then, they've lightened up a bit or lost that respect for each other, especially during informal matches, like this one.

During the whole event, no one talked to Dianna, as if she wasn't there. They all knew that Captain Boofy's wife, Lorelei, didn't want her there. They sympathized with Lorelei. They must have sensed her feelings. Back then, people could sense each other's feelings, which only a few of us can do today. And so the whole match was not nearly as much fun to the participants and their families as other matches had been. There was a sense of tenseness in the air that everyone seemed to pick up on. Captain Boofy tried not to notice it and acted as joyful and frisky as he did at previous matches, but he was the only one that acted okay.

Dianna was too busy enjoying the watching to notice the tense atmosphere. She was just glad to be there and to see how well Captain Boofy does at archery. And, of course, she clapped her hands in joy whenever he'd hit the middle of the target, especially at the end, when he fired another arrow, which split the arrow that was already there, in half. Then she stood up and clapped, yelling, "Yaaaay!"

At that moment, Captain Boofy's wife, Lorelei, overheard her and turned around, giving Dianna a look that "kills a thousand men". So Dianna sat down. She was embarrassed and sorry that she cheered too loud. She got a little carried away.

Captain Boofy's wife, Lorelei, furiously ran onto the field and grabbed his hand and yanked him off the field, yelling, "Come-on, Josefitos, we're going home! I can't stand it here any longer!" Captain Boofy let his wife drag him home and he reluctantly went with her, although he wanted to stop by the club house for a brew after the match, but it looked like Lorelei wasn't going to let him do that this night.

Chapter 5 B

That night, Dianna had a nightmare. She dreamed that she saw a ship in the middle of the ocean. It appeared to be sinking. The name on it was "Andrea".

A few months later, a rumor went around that the ship builders had finished the new luxury cruise ship they had been working on and were to baptize it on a certain day, in spring, most likely on Spring Festival Day.

When that day came, the dock of Altronia was crowded with people --- women and men in their best robes, and children, too --- all dressed up, trying to make the most positive impression on each other. Everyone watched the King baptize the ship. Dianna arrived late, and ran, pushing her way through the crowd until she got close enough to recognize the name on the ship. It was "Andrea"!

Seconds after she arrived, they cut the rope barring the entrance ramp to the ship. People who were lined up behind it started boarding the ship. Dianna watched in horror as she remembered the nightmare or premonition she had a few moons ago. She fought her way through the crowd until she reached the ramp, walked up to King Seabourne and said, "Please --- don't let the people on the ship!

The King turned around and looked down on her and said, "Why shouldn't I?"

"It's gonna sink! I know it! I had a premonition!"

"That is preposterous!" said the King.

"*Please*, Your Highness, listen to me!" begged Dianna. "I'm telling you: it's gonna sink, it's gonna … really, it will! I saw it in my dream!" She turned to the crowd outside the ship and cried, "Please! Listen to me! I'm telling you: it *will* sink!"

But all her pleading was in vain. Neither King Seabourne nor the people listened to her or believed her. No one did. They just kept on boarding that ship. Soon, a guard pulled Dianna aside and asked, "May I see your ticket?"

"No, I don't have a ticket, I'm not …" was all Dianna could say before he interrupted her with "What makes you think you can board the ship without a ticket?!" But Dianna didn't want to get on that ship. She was just trying to warn people about a possible mishap that would involve the ship. However, the guard wouldn't listen to her and just tossed her aside.

She landed against a boulder, broke down, and cried. Then she got up and tried it again. This time, she was so full of emotion that she screamed at the people in the line that was moving onto the ramp at a moderate pace. "Please, don't get on that ship! It'll sink!" she cried. "I had a nightmare about this! I had a premonition!"

But the people only looked at her as if she was crazy. And again she was whisked away by the guards. They carried her away while she kicked and screamed and cried. She also called to Captain Boofy, when she saw him, "Captain Boofy! PLEASE! Get off that ship! It'll sink! It really will! I beg of you, please, get off that ship!"

But he probably was in a place on the ship where he couldn't even hear her. Dianna feared that something might happen to him, that he may never return! The guards tied her up and brought her to their headquarters where they locked her in a tiny room for the rest of the time that ship was on its trip. She sat in there and cried violently.

And so all the people who were supposed to sail on the new luxury cruise ship "Andrea" boarded and were now sailing peacefully into the sunset, without any notion of what was to come. The adults chatted while the children happily chased each other around. Everyone was enjoying their vacation trip. Everything went according to plan --- until after all the guests and most of the crew went to sleep.

Suddenly there was a lightning bolt in the sky, followed shortly by a huge thunder --- and then the sky opened up, letting out the worst rainstorm they ever experienced. The rain came down in buckets. One of the sailors, the one that was steering the ship, ran into Captain Boofy's sleeping quarters, exclaiming, "Captain, there's a bad storm raging! A lightning bolt hit one of the masts, and it caught on fire!" While the sailor awoke Captain Boofy, and while they were running to the deck, with Captain Boofy's eyes small at first, when he awoke, but growing to their usual large size as he arrived on deck, the top of the mast came down in flames. It crashed down on the ship deck, hitting one of the other sailors. Seeing that, Captain Boofy quickly grabbed a bucket of water and a box of salt, yelling to the sailors to get more water, blankets, and salt, and put out the fire. Then he said, "There. I hope the fire didn't damage the ship too much!"

But the fire already burnt a hole in the deck by the time it was out and that woke up the passengers below. So they stated panicking and all headed to one end of the ship, causing the other end to rise. Then it happened that a huge tidal wave rolled under the high end of the ship, which *almost* caused it to turn over! A few people who were already on the low end of the ship went overboard, screaming, and drowned. But the reason the ship didn't turn over is because Captain Boofy ordered all the sailors to take some ballast stones, and anything else heavy they came across, and take it over to the high end of the ship *immediately,* while he grabbed the steering wheel and spun it to one side, steering the ship in a different direction. That seemed to change the ship's mind about turning over and sinking.

Eventually the storm died, or the ship sailed out of the storm, and the remaining people were relieved that they survived. The sailor on whom the mast fell was lying in his cot, where they carried him to, after Captain Boofy lifted the burning mast off of him. He healed his burned hands later, using a crystal. The sailor now had a massive burn on his back, which would also be healed at the healing temple with a crystal, but for now, he was in a coma but still alive.

The ship had some broken sails and masts to be repaired as well as the hole in the deck. Captain Boofy ordered the sailors to repair the ship as best as they could without a fresh supply of wood or cloth or anything else, until they returned to Altronia Harbor for the grand overhaul, as the ship was badly damaged by the storm.

As the people disembarked the ship, they kissed the ground as the crowd cheered. Someone said to Captain Boofy, "Captain Boofy, you amaze me, the way you managed to keep the ship from sinking! If it wasn't for you, we'd all have drowned!"

"Thanks!" was all he said.

Chapter 6

As soon as the ship "Andrea" returned, the authorities set Dianna free. She went home to watch on her TV screen what happened to the ship. She watched in horror as it showed how the ship looked when it returned to Altronia and the horrified expressions on the faces of some of the people who sailed on it and how some of the ladies were holding their hand on their hearts. Others were crying while trying to tell their stories. The worst thing was that she knew this was going to happen, and somehow she felt that she didn't try hard enough to warn them. The trouble was: she did try to warn them profusely, but they just refused to listen to her. Nevertheless, she was glad that Captain Boofy had saved the ship and returned alive and well.

The authorities told Dianna to take a few days off from her work and rest until she'd get over what happened to the ship, the passengers, and her. But she had a lot of work to do, and the deadline was drawing near, so she flew over to Altronia to get it done.

But when she arrived, the natives were not as friendly as they used to be. As she arrived at the house she was working on, the dwellers treated her with cold shoulders. When she went to the local restaurant, the Kiva Nova, for lunch, the waitress there greeted her with a mean look on her face. After Dianna bought her meal, she saw her friends, including Captain Boofy, sitting over there in a certain corner. But there were 2 women sitting with them who she's never seen before. The Monkey was sitting there, too.

Dianna said, "Hi guys!"

But the "Friends" only looked up long enough to say, "Mft…"

And when Dianna went over to them, they wouldn't let her sit with them. So she said, "What's the matter? Can't I sit with you guys?"

"No, why don't you go sit over there and eat your lunch?" suggested Monkey.

"Aw come-on," begged Dianna. "You've been letting me sit with you guys for the last few months. Why not today?"

"**NO!**" bellowed Monkey so loud, even people outside of the restaurant could hear him. Dianna was shocked. She had never heard him yell like that before.

Trembling from the sound of that, she mustered up enough strength to ask, "But … but why?"

With a stern look on his face and his index finger pointing at Dianna, Monkey continued to yell at Dianna, "And if you ever let Lorelei see you near Captain Boofy again, she'll slap your face!"

"Oh! Is that what this is about!" Dianna yelled back. "But it seems alright for those 2 women to sit with you guys, huh?!"

None of the people sitting at that table answered. Half of the 4 just raised their heads a little, but only for half a second before they lowered them again and returned to eating.

So Dianna had to eat her lunch by herself in another, unoccupied, corner on the other side of the room.

Later on, in the afternoon, when Dianna was done with her work for the day and getting ready to fly to Atlantis, she ran into Captain Boofy (figuratively). He asked her in the usual friendly voice, "How are you?"

Dianna smiled in relief, as she had feared that he, too, would be unfriendly to her, just like the rest of the people on Altronia. She answered with a sigh, "I don't understand it, no one is talking to me today! Everyone is giving me the cold shoulder and some people were even threatening me! What's up with this place? Did they have a look-alike of mine in a scary movie or something? What's going on here?"

Then Captain Boofy answered, "It's because of what happened to the new ship." he explained. "They saw you at the baptizing service the other day. Now they think you caused that storm to happen because you were upset about not being allowed to board the ship."

"What? You've got to be kidding!" was all Dianna could say at that moment.

Captain Boofy shook his head and said, "They think you cast a spell on the new ship, using one of your crystals."

Dianna was hugely dismayed. She stood there with her mouth open. "But … but I wasn't trying to get on that ship! I didn't want a free ride! I was trying to warn everyone that I had a dream --- a nightmare --- that this ship was sinking! But nobody would listen to me! Instead, they locked me up in a prison cell! You know, the kind they used to keep criminals in! Oh please, Captain Boofy," she begged him, "spread the word that I didn't put a spell on the ship. I got a premonition and I tried to warn everyone against boarding that ship, but they <u>would not let me!</u>"

"I believe you!" said Captain Boofy.

Then she added, "Are you sure that's the only reason?" It wasn't.

"There is another reason," said Captain Boofy. "It's because you went to my archery contest the other day. My wife got very upset about that."

Since Captain Boofy was a very honorable man, among the workers, everyone looked up to him, and everyone believed what he said. Of course, since he was an honest man, they had no reason to disbelieve him about anything. So, if he would have told people that Dianna was not trying to get a free ride on the ship "Andrea", but was trying to save the ship from impending doom, the people would have believed him and continued to be friendly with her.

But Captain Boofy talked it over with his wife, before telling anyone anything, because he usually talks things over with his wife before he makes a decision.

As soon as she heard the name Dianna, she started yelling, "What? Are you talking about that B…. who's after you?"

"But Lorelei, she's just a … "interjected Captain Boofy."

"No way!" Lorelei interrupted him. "Don't you dare tell them anything nice about her!" she yelled. "If I find out you told them what she told you or that you're even thinking of telling them, I'll divorce you and take the baby with me!"

"Oh no, don't do that to me!" Captain Boofy cried.

"Then heed my words and don't tell anyone about Dianna! She don't deserve to have anyone on this island talk to her!! She don't even have no business here, that marriage breaker, she should stay in Atlantis, where she belongs!"

"Oh, so that's it!" yelled Captain Boofy. "You're still not over seeing us talking the other day, huh?"

"It's not just that!" yelled Lorelei. "She couldn't even stay away from that archery contest of yours!"

So that's how she talked him out of sticking up for Dianna. And therefore, the truth never came out and the people were left in the wrong belief. So from that day on, hardly anyone on that island of Altronia ever talked to Dianna again.

Dianna was going to leave Altronia forever that day, if it weren't for the Annual Altronia Picnic.

Every year, during Altronia's beautiful and warm spring season, the natives of the island put on an annual picnic. This was called The Annual Altronia Picnic. Dianna would go to this fun event each year, especially this one year that she knew Captain Boofy would be there. She figured it would be a fun event and was looking forward to it. King Seabourne, who put it on, would always provide a long smorgasbord of luscious, free food, which included plenty of Lemuria's delicious fruits of all kinds and vegetables that weren't bitter, as well as freshly-made pies and other sweets and breads from Atlantis' bakeries, and, of course, delicious barbeque of the finest beef and chicken, hot dogs, and hamburgers, or the equivalent thereof.

Everyone that lived or worked on that island, or had relatives, business relations, or friends there, attended this festival each year. And so Dianna made sure she didn't miss it this year, either.

Since everyone was allowed to bring their family members along, Dianna brought her sister and her nephew, who were the only family members she still had around. Her mother was out of town, and her brother was in the Atlantean Service, which took him to another colony of Atlantis or country. But her sister was available at that time, so she and her son went with Dianna to the picnic.

When Dianna and her relatives arrived, there were already a lot of people bustling about, having fun. Children were running around, grown-ups were talking to each other and eating the delicious food. Captain Boofy and his wife were sitting together under one of the palm trees with their baby laying in a basket just his size between them. Captain Boofy was leaning up against the tree while Lorelei was hunched over, chewing on a turkey leg. Dianna spotted them shortly after she and her relatives arrived. When she saw their little one, she went right up to them and looked at the small child in wonder. She said, "Wow, is that your baby?"

"Yup." said Captain Boofy.

"Wow!" exclaimed Dianna again. "He looks adorable!" She noticed that their baby had very unusually wide almond-shaped eyes, probably from his dad. She did remember Captain Boofy saying once, "He looks like me!" proudly.

Captain Boofy and his wife weren't too pleased to see Dianna. Nevertheless, she proceeded to introduce her sister and nephew to them. "This is my sister, Marlena, and my nephew, Julius. Marlena, that is Captain Boofy who is the captain of the ship C.S. Altronia, and that is his wife, Lorelei, and the little one is their baby."

Captain Boofy managed to squeeze out a weak "Hello." while Lorelei only let a "Humph." out of her. So much for formal introductions.

Later on, King Seabourne organized a primitive version of today's baseball game, (maybe it was cricket or something) for families to play. They used a thinner, stick-like bat and a small rubber ball, a smaller version of what they used for hipball. They had the picnic near a citadel, so they used that as a field. Incidentally, that field was sometimes also used for hipball games and it had a vertical cement ring hanging high up on the wall for that purpose.

Dianna played, too. She has had some experience playing that kind of game. She has said to several of the natives of Altronia, "I'd rather play it than watch!" Her sister, however, declined to play. She had hardly any contact with the Altronians or anybody else that was there, except her own son. This was even though she was known in Dianna's family as an outgoing girl who loved to talk.

This type of baseball was an ancient game that was later played in Egypt, one of Atlantis' colonies, by Egyptian pharos, with their priests as catchers. This may have been an ancient precursor to baseball, softball, and even stickball. As the "basebol" game got under way and the teams had been picked, Monkey saw Dianna's glove and noticed that it wasn't exactly newly bought from the neighborhood sports store, that it was a little stiff, (it actually has been around for a few years). Since Dianna was not exactly rich, she couldn't afford to buy a brand new glove just for this one game. So he made fun of her old glove, saying, "That glove looks like it belongs in a museum!"

Dianna ended up on the opposite team of Captain Boofy. There was someone else pitching when she first went up to bat. He threw the ball several times, but Dianna refused to swing the bat, because she could sense that he was trying to strike her out. The ball didn't look like it was in her swinging range for her to hit it. So the other players grew impatient. They wanted to strike her out as quickly as possible.

So Dianna was trying to get to walk to first base, which she would get to do, if the pitcher throws 4 foul balls. However, after the 3rd pitch, Captain Boofy intervened and took over the pitcher's duties temporarily. He threw the ball practically right towards Dianna's bat. She watched the ball come to her intently --- and swung the bat --- and hit it! It went right to the ground and rolled past Captain Boofy into the center outfield as she dropped the bat and ran as fast as she could to first base. By the time the center outfield player got a hold of the ball and threw it to Captain Boofy, Dianna had made it to first base, her heart beating wildly. Some of the people cheered, among them, her sister, but not many others. Nevertheless, Dianna was proud of herself having made it to first base and thankful (only in thought) to Captain Boofy for having pitched the ball right to her bat.

Later on, two more batters hit the ball, which sent Dianna to second and third base, but the third batter struck out, and since that was the 3rd out already, the teams had to switch, and Dianna never made it to home plate. Oh well… Monkey called over to the 3rd batter, "Joey, you struck out! What good are you?!"

Soon after the end of the "basebol" game, the picnic event was over, and everybody went home. Dianna and her relatives left, too, without saying good-bye to anyone.

After the Altronia Picnic day, Dianna didn't expect to see anyone from that island ever again. Her assignment was completed and she got paid and no one gave her any new assignments. So she had no reason to go back there again. However, she did see Captain Boofy once more, when he docked his ship in Poseidon Harbor while she happened to be there on errands. They greeted each other as usual. She said, "You sure have an adorable child!

He agreed proudly, "Thank you!"

Then she told him the sad news: "Captain Boofy, I regret to tell you, I can't see you anymore."

"You can't?" he said, surprised, "But why?" he asked.

Dianna responded, "Because of what happened. I haven't got a single assignment from your island since that day. You see, my reputation is ruined. And if they catch us speaking together, they'll probably hang us both!"

"No they won't!" assured Captain Boofy in disbelief.

Dianna continued, "I was thinking of killing myself …"

"Aw c'mon, don't do that to me!" said Captain Boofy.

"Well," she said, "if I didn't know I would have to return to this planet with a much worse life, I probably would have done it, but …" she turned to him and looked deeply into his wide, almond-shaped, dark eyes, "Please understand: I don't want anyone to hurt you!"

For a second or two, their eyes met. Then he looked away and said, "I gotta load these boxes up. Care to help me?"

Dianna smiled and said, "Sure!"

They loaded the boxes onto the ship conveyor belt together. One box was stuck to the ground for some reason, or it was particularly heavy, on Dianna's side. So he said, coaxingly, "Come-on!"

That gave Dianna the extra adrenalin she needed, and she picked up her end of the box. She knew he was kidding, which is why she smiled and gave it a good tug, which worked.

They finished loading the boxes sooner than she wanted, and it was time for him to leave. Dianna said, "One more thing I'd like to know: Why were those 2 women allowed to sit with you guys at the Kiva Nova the other day, when I wasn't? They are not married to neither of you, are they?"

Captain Boofy answered matter-of-factly, "They're friends of Lorelei."

So Dianna walked home and Captain Boofy sailed away into the sunset, to Altronia.

Chapter 7

On the island of Altronia, as well as on Atlantis, history was changing. The Golden Age came to an abrupt end when either earthquakes or a comet or the combination thereof hit and sank Lemuria. For a while after that, the people of both Altronia and Atlantis were shocked. From then on, some of them started doubting whom they were venerating and some of the people started being less spiritual and more materialistic. The people basically split up into two groups: the Children of the Law of One, who were still spiritual, and the Sons of Belial, who were the materialistic ones. This latter group took things for granted. They started taking advantage of things, and of each other. The worst of them started turning away from God and worshipping themselves by having sculptures made in their own likeness. These people were so land hungry that they were constantly at war with other countries, like Greece, Turkey, Iberia (we know it as Spain), and Egypt. They wanted to gain control over what was occupied by the Children of One as well. They were colonizing land everywhere and never getting enough. Also, when any of their colonies wanted to become their own countries, the Sons of Belial would make war against them and do whatever it took to cause earthquakes in that colony to keep its people under their control.

Among the Children of the Law of One were the priests and priestesses and their followers. These people held onto the traditional monotheistic religion that the Atlanteans have been taught from a long time ago. On Atlantis, Dianna was one of the followers of the Children of One. On Altronia, King Seabourne, the royal family, and Captain Boofy were all followers of the Children of One, while Lorelei, Monkey, and Athol, were on the side of the Sons of Belial. The rest of the Altronians were split right down the middle. Half of them were Children of One and the other half were Sons of Belial.

On Atlantis, as well as on all of its colonies, they regularly had bull fighting rituals. They had the same thing on Altronia. These rituals were similar to the bull fights people are enjoying today in the southwestern part of the US, Spain, and Mexico. Today's bull fighting games may have come from these ancient lands.

At every bullfighting ritual, King Seabourne would show up with his family. They would sit in a special box in the amphitheater and watch with excitement. He would also announce at the beginning of the games, "Let the games begin!"

And so the games began this day, which set out to be a beautiful day with perfect weather and good-natured people. But unfortunately, it did not end this way. King Seabourne was enjoying an exciting game of bullfighting up to a certain time, when his daughter, Poinsettia, who sat next to him, suddenly let out a shrill scream. She saw her father's head abruptly drop forward. It happened just when she was asking him a question. At that bloody sight, she was screaming hysterically. She alerted her mother, and then there were two women screaming and crying. No one knew who did it. The news spread throughout the crowd all around the amphitheater like wildfire. Everyone cried out in horror! "The King is dead!" a voice cried out here and there. "Oh no!" people gasped everywhere. Most people couldn't understand why anyone would want to assassinate the King, especially since he was a very respectable king. But some people were either well read, listened well in politics, or just instinctly knew something like this would happen sooner or later. However, even they were surprised that this happened so soon. They never found out who did it, but it must have been one of the Sons of Belial who coveted the King's throne and wanted to be Altronia's next king. The assassin ran away immediately, but he didn't get very far before someone else killed him with an arrow shot in his back. That killer immediately grabbed the King's murderer and threw him in the ocean for shark food. The assassin's murderer didn't want anyone to find out that he killed anyone, so he cleaned up his tracks so well that no one ever suspected that he murdered the murderer of the King. Then he defected from the island and moved to Atlantis. The King's throne, which was now up for grabs, was momentarily occupied by the King's wife, until Princess Poinsettia would become old enough to take over. She was still too young to take over the throne at this point.

And so this day's bullfighting game ended on a horrible note. The Queen decided that from here on out, there'll be no more bullfighting rituals on Altronia. The Princess wouldn't have them, either. But on Atlantis, as well as on all the colonies thereof, the bullfighting rituals continued, right up to the present day in whichever countries still exist.

Chapter 8

On the C.S. Altronia, Captain Boofy was steering the ship. Suddenly one of his sailors ran to him, yelling, "Captain Boofy! There's another ship coming – and it doesn't look friendly!"

"Let me see!" said Captain Boofy seriously, grabbing the looking glass. As he removed them, his eyes were wide with fury. "It is Monkey! And he's heading straight for us!"

Captain Boofy and Monkey haven't been getting along too well lately, ever since the society started splitting up into the Children of One and the Sons of Belial. Monkey had learned how to navigate a ship from Captain Boofy when he sailed aboard his ship (the C.S. Altronia) and was taught during peaceful times before the split in society.

Now that Captain Boofy saw Monkey's ship coming, he quickly assembled his crew and told them to prepare in high speed for war. His men were strong and healthy and had learned martial arts a long time ago, just incase the day would come when another ship would attack them. So did Monkey's men, and they were strong and healthy, too. Captain Boofy's crew haven't had the need to fight anyone in many years, so now they verbally went over their moves at lightning speed while they donned their protective gear and picked up their weapons. They didn't have much time to get prepared as Monkey's ship was approaching fast.

In minutes it arrived and Monkey's men were jumping onto the C.S. Altronia and fighting with Captain Boofy's men. First they used swords, then, when the swords would get knocked out of the hands, they used martial arts. They used lethal moves for they were fighting each other to kill. The fighting was hard and long and many sailors were killed on both sides. At first it looked like Captain Boofy and his men were winning, but then their luck turned on them. Monkey's men were gaining ground, killing more and more of Captain Boofy's men.

Captain Boofy himself was busy, fighting at least two men at a time. He was doing pretty good – until all the sailors were laying around and dead on both sides and only Captain Boofy and Monkey were left still living.

Now it was two ex-friends that were turned into bitter enemies by the evils of politics facing each other and Monkey had only one intention in mind. First they fenced with swords. That went on for a while. Then Monkey knocked Captain Boofy's sword out of his hand. Thinking he's got him now, Monkey put a lusty smile on his face and threw his sword, pointy end first, at Captain Boofy's chest. But Captain Boofy jumped to the side, did a summersault, and jumped on Monkey. They wrestled for a while with Captain Boofy hitting Monkey in the chest with a left hook and then a right hook, which sent the latter reeling backwards 20 cubits.

Then Monkey got up and picked up a wooden 4 by 4, which he swung at Captain Boofy, who ducked in the last second. Then he grabbed the other end of the board and swung it at Monkey. But he ducked, too. And then they attacked each other and wrestled. Captain Boofy grabbed a lamp and hit Monkey over the head with it. Then Monkey found a vase that he used on Captain Boofy. Then they chased each other to the other end of the ship and wrestled some more there. Captain Boofy had another sword hidden under some supplies there. He retrieved that and swung it at Monkey, shaving off a bit of his shoulder, but only a small piece of skin, yet enough to make him bleed. But Monkey also managed to find a sword somewhere nearby and charged with it at Captain Boofy. But the latter rolled over so that the former missed. By now, Captain Boofy was growing weary and had lost one ear and was bleeding from that side of his head. He had just enough strength to pick up an empty chest and toss it at Monkey, who by then had lost sight in one of his eyes. The chest threw Monkey back and landed on top of him, knocking him out for a few seconds.

Captain Boofy thought Monkey was dead and started to walk away. But Monkey was still alive, so while Captain Boofy took his eyes off of him, he got up secretly and was charging at Captain Boofy from behind with an open pocketknife. In the last second, Captain Boofy turned around to find Monkey heading towards him. By then, the former was near the railing of the ship. So he simply stepped aside and, using his hands and his foot, helped Monkey continue heading in the same direction. And so Monkey fell overboard into the sea. Then, to make sure he wouldn't return, Captain Boofy fired an arrow at him and got him right in the back. Now Monkey tried to swim towards the ship, but he was bleeding out of more than one hole in his body and head, and there just happened to be a school of sharks coming along. When they found him, they made a meal out of him.

By then, all of Monkey's men and all of Captain Boofy's men had died in battle. After watching the sharks finish off Monkey, Captain Boofy fired a Malakoff at Monkey's ship, the Routier, and watched it burn. The flames reached sky-high before she sank into the ocean, never to be found again. Then he went down into the hull to nurse his wounds to heal. After that, he sailed his ship, the C.S. Altronia to America. He heard that the crystal makers or miners were looking for some new men to help them, so he decided after that almost fatal event that he didn't want anything further to do with being a captain and manning a ship. He was also tired of his wife and the whole life on Altronia. So he migrated to where the crystal quarries were, somewhere in what is now southeastern United States, and got a job mining or making crystals for Atlantis.

Meanwhile, on Atlantis, Dianna stood at the dock of Poseidon, watching the ships depart and arrive, wondering whether Captain Boofy might sail into the harbor. She wasn't planning on seeing him, as she had already told him that she wasn't going to see him anymore, as she couldn't stand the way the people were looking at her and treating her, as if she had committed adultery, just for being in love with him, something she couldn't help, just for going to his game, something she could have avoided. They never did anything together, except talk, work, and eat. And there is absolutely nothing wrong with that, and she never wanted it to go any further. But once word spread around like wildfire about her attending that archery contest, …

"Here ye, here ye!" cried a courier boy nearby. "Read all about it! The C.S. Altronia has been attacked by pirates!"

'Attacked!' she thought, 'What happened? Is Captain Boofy all right?' she wondered, as she ran over to the boy to buy a copy scroll off of him. Then she sat down on a stairway nearby, unrolled the scroll, and read the headline story. It said, "C.S. Altronia has been attacked. The captain was attacked by a pirate and killed, and so was all of the crew. Neither ship nor sailor has been seen since."

'It was Monkey!' she realized. 'What an a..hole! How could he do that to his best friend?' She knew they had been on different sides, but she never dreamed it would come to this! 'This is horrible!' she thought and began to cry. She never stopped crying for 3 weeks. After all that crying, she had to regenerate her face, as it suffered from all those tears. She also had to go to a professional therapist to help her get over him and move on with her life. It was a great struggle, as for months she didn't feel like doing anything, not even getting out of bed. Every time she'd see anyone that looked anywhere near like Captain Boofy, she'd relapse into another depression. He was, and would always be, the most beautiful and the nicest man she'd ever seen.

Chapter 9

Meanwhile on Atlantis, the people have clearly split into 2 groups and the Sons of Belial were already giving the Children of One a hard time. There were often drive-by shootings. Every now and then, a riot broke out. Sometimes the Sons of Belial would set one of the buildings of the Children of One on fire. Every now and then, somebody disappeared (meaning they were assassinated). The High Priests, who still ruled one part of Atlantis officially, were losing power, as the Sons of Belial simply wouldn't heed their word, and basically did whatever they wanted. So the priests, who were Children of One, were regarded as figureheads. Eventually, they and their followers were driven north into the mountains by the Sons of Belial.

One day, at about 12:00 noon, as business in downtown Poseidon went on as usual, and as on Altronia guerilla wars were breaking out among the groups, a soft rumble was heard that grew louder and louder. Athol, who had in the meantime managed to move himself up to head of the Altronia Construction Company somehow, had his favorite of 7 beautiful secretaries sitting on his lap, taking a "dictation".

Suddenly the BIG ONE hit Altronia (earthquake)! The building Athol was in started shaking. Other buildings were collapsing, including the PC manufacturing plant. Fire broke out everywhere! People were screaming! Athol's Construction Company's office building was built just recently with all the precautions. That didn't do the people inside a single bit of good now.

"What was that?" asked the secretary.

"I dunno. Let's hurry up and get this letter written!" said Athol.

Athol and his secretary got frightened at first. The secretary went to the window of the penthouse where Athol had his office and looked out. She saw the volcano way off in the distance. It wasn't looking too good.

"Look!" she exclaimed. "Mount Abba is pregnant! It looks like it's about to burst!"

"Don't worry 'bout it, Honey, we're on the highest floor, and I made this building tough enough to weather anything." said Athol. "We'll just ride it out."

But the shaking did not cease. Instead, it got increasingly violent. Suddenly Mount Abba burst open and lava shot out the side, quickly covering everything between it and Athol's building and lighting everything in its path on fire. Soon it reached Athol's indestructible office building and it was suddenly engulfed in a wall of flames, scorching everything, even the quartz marble floors. It melted it in seconds and turned it all into flames.

As Athol's office was getting hotter and hotter, his secretary took off, slamming the door shut behind her. It was the only door to his office. Athol tried to get out, but the door was locked and the ladder was already on fire. He ran to the window and yelled and screamed for his secretary to get another ladder, but in vain. He could have jumped out, but was afraid to, since the building was now surrounded by molten rock and fire. It was a long, long way down from his penthouse office, and he didn't have the gadget to summon his chariot, either. The window also wasn't big enough for him to fit his large body through. So he punched the wall next to it to enlarge the window. That caused the ceiling to collapse on him, pinning him to the floor. As he looked up toward the window, he saw that some of the wall had fallen away and the window was now big enough for him to jump out. But now that the block of stone from the ceiling was on top of him, he couldn't move. The flames started to come through the opening in the floor as that started to melt. Athol did not lose consciousness. He was screaming as the flames began to lick at his body. Then his clothes caught on fire, and eventually his face and hair. But he still did not lose consciousness.

Eventually the building collapsed and was covered with the lava that was surrounding it. The whole thing went down and Athol went down with it, screaming all the way.

Then the huge 100 cubit tidal waves came and washed over the island of Altronia, drowning everyone who was still alive, except for the very few people who managed to find rescue ships and had climbed into them. And Captain Boofy's wife, Lorelei, was in one of the smaller ones with her son, who had just celebrated his first birthday. She knew that her boat wasn't going to make it in the turbulent sea. But there was a larger ship nearby of a design similar to a canoe that was able to survive completely under water. Her husband had told her of ships like that just before he abducted to America. This ship was above water at the time and its crew was telling the people in the rescue boats to throw them their babies so they could take them to Atlantis, so they can survive.

So in the last minute, she threw her son through the air to one of the crew who caught him just before a huge wave buried that whole boat that she was in, taking all of its passengers down into the abyss. Then another even bigger tidal wave closed in over Altronia, as it sank, shutting the door on the existence of that island forever.

Chapter 10

When the people on Atlantis found out about the demise of Altronia from a flying aircraft rider, they were horrified. The aircraft pilot had a video camera aboard and made use of it right away. When he returned, he took the film to the TV station people. They were shocked! They sent 2 of their reporters out there in a ship. The next day they came back and said they could not get anywhere near where the island was.

"There was such a huge pile of pumice, ash, shoal, and mud that the entire area where Altronia had been was impassable! We had to turn back." said the reporters, "We did see a huge reddish-black cloud hovering over the area."

They said it couldn't happen, but it did! This event slowed down the riots and other outbreaks on Atlantis, as both sides realized that the Altronians have caused their island to sink by their guerilla wars, by bombs bursting into the air, destroying not only buildings and people, but also the whole island itself. It also destroyed the whole computer industry.

Dianna was stunned when she heard about the inundation of Altronia. By then, she was suffering from chronic stomach aches (maybe from stress, or maybe she was psychic enough to pick up on the mass of people suddenly drowning as the island was being covered with lava and then ocean water). She had heard in social circles about the use of crystals for healing, so she acquired herself a rose quartz crystal and tried it. It worked quite well, to her amazement. So she went to the University of Atlantis and took up "Healing through Crystals". She did so well that her teacher said she was psychic. After a few weeks, she discovered she could even heal people with her bare hands. As she took more classes and got some serious training at the advice of her master, she started to see auras around people and also became clairvoyant.

She would record her dream in a voice box, every time she had one. After a while, she had quite a collection of dreams and she began to decipher them. Oftentimes, her dreams told her the future.

After a few years, Dianna's master took her with him to the old priests up North, in the mountains. The priests used to govern the island of Atlantis before they were driven into the mountains by the Sons of Belial. These priests taught her religion as well as refined her powers and they made her give a solemn promise never to misuse them. She studied under these priests for 7 years.

When Dianna was finished with her training, she returned to Poseidon to find out to her fright that politics have changed drastically while she was gone. They have become a whole lot worse. Women were abused; children were mishandled and neglected, and committing suicide in huge numbers. And people only cared about money and were more selfish than ever. And corruption was going on everywhere.

So Dianna started a group to improve things. The group grew in number and power. Eventually they were able to take back the leadership in Atlantis. When they did, they made Dianna into a priestess. She reigned along with the other priests for many years. She had a circle of advisors who helped her make the right decisions by giving her advice. She noticed that one of the guys in that circle looked very familiar. She could have sworn he looked very similar to Captain Boofy. Could it be his son?

THE END

Printed in the United States
by Baker & Taylor Publisher Services